Zena A Maher

Witch Hypnotizer

Zena A Maher

Witch Hypnotizer

ISBN/EAN: 9783337394684

Printed in Europe, USA, Canada, Australia, Japan

Cover: Foto ©Andreas Hilbeck / pixelio.de

More available books at **www.hansebooks.com**

THE
WITCH HYPNOTIZER

✳

BY

ZENA A. MAHER

✳

PUBLISHED FOR THE AUTHOR

SAN FRANCISCO
THE BANCROFT COMPANY
1892

BY

ZENA A. MAHER

Issued from the Press of
THE BANCROFT COMPANY

✳

To My Husband,
the Truest and Noblest of Men

THE WITCH HYPNOTIZER

CHAPTER I.

Let there be light. Genesis i, 3.
Let your light so shine before men, that they may see your good works, and glorify your Father which is in Heaven. Matthew v, 16.

In the world of imagination many Witches have lived and died since the one of whose existence and wonders I am about to relate, came into prominence.

She lived quite alone in a little cottage on the outskirts of a large city in America, of course, and why should not the free soil produce all sorts when it is the dumping ground for all creation?

Alone, with the exception of her dog and several cages of canaries which, by the way, were a new departure in the line of pets, for the old-time Witches were supposed to favor cats and parrots, she commanded the respect of all, but there was something so very peculiar about her that some of her more superstitious neighbors looked upon this woman as a kind of good Witch.

There was nothing remarkable about her personal appearance and the peculiarity was not visibly noticeable. It was nothing tangible, but an indescribable something which gave her influence over other minds, to bend them to her will.

Every one felt this more or less in her presence; a giving up of pet hobbies, even, to her ideas, which fortunately were very liberal.

There was that also about her sympathetic nature which invited confidence, and many who were not given to complaining found themselves, they hardly knew why, telling her their secret sorrows.

For years this Witch or woman was herself unconscious of this power, but when she fully realized it, her work to her conscientious heart was laid out, and that must be in doing all the good possible through this genius that was hers.

She had always endeavored to do her best, ever ready to lend a helping hand to any one in trouble.

CHAPTER II.

While attending to her birds one morning, the Witch was interrupted by a knock at the door and a summons from one of her neighbors, who had sent a child to ask if this good soul would come over.

Yes, she would be there directly.

Donning her sombre colored bonnet and shawl the Witch started for her neighbor's. The unhappy little woman craved sympathy, and had sent for her who knew so well how to render it.

She told the oft-repeated story of a drunkard's wife. Her husband had left home the previous evening and had not returned, and after these prolonged sprees she feared his coming, who was the kindest of men when himself, but very savage when under the influence of liquor. Then, too, she was afraid that he would lose his position, which his employer had threatened if he did not attend to work better.

The Witch told her to be of good cheer; that all would be well with her yet.

She looked at the shabby furniture and still shabbier clothing of the children. This family had once been in comfortable circumstances, but were brought to this state of poverty through intemperance, the prevailing evil.

For the drunkard and the glutton shall come to poverty. Proverbs, xxiii, 21.

And yet how much good these beverages might do if used in moderation, but too many are with this, like all their other appetites over which they have no control. The mind should be made to strive harder after the knowledge of God in order to subdue these carnal desires.

For they that are after the flesh do mind the things of the flesh: but they that are after the Spirit, the things of the Spirit.
For to be carnally minded is death; but to be spiritually minded is life and peace.
Because the carnal mind is enmity against God; for it is not subject to the law of God, neither indeed can be.
So then they that are in the flesh cannot please God.
As many as are led by the Spirit of God, they are the sons of God Romans viii, 5, 6, 7, 8, 14.
Woe unto them that rise up early in the morning, that they may follow strong drink, that continue until night, till wine inflame them!
Woe unto them that are mighty to drink wine, and men of strength to mingle strong drink. Isaiah v, 11, 22.

He that soweth to his flesh shall of the flesh reap corruption; but he that soweth to the Spirit shall of the Spirit reap life everlasting. Galatians vi. 8.

All things indeed are pure; but it is evil for that man who eateth with offense.

It is good neither to eat flesh, nor to drink wine, nor anything whereby thy brother stumbleth, or is offended, or is made weak. Romans xiv, 20, 21.

Whilst we are at home in the body, we are absent from the Lord. II Corinthians v, 6.

Be not drunk with wine wherein is excess; but be filled with the Spirit. Ephesians v, 18.

Walk in the Spirit and ye shall not fulfill the lust of the flesh. Galatians v, 16.

Denying ungodliness and worldly lusts, we should live soberly, righteously and godly in this present world. Titus ii, 12.

About midday this fallen image of God came home partially sobered and ferocious as a wild animal. The Witch mentally compared man with beast and gave her dog the preference.

He had commenced his wicked profanity, when a hand was laid on his arm and reproachful eyes looked into his.

Wine is a mocker, strong drink is raging; and whoever is deceived thereby is not wise. Proverbs xx, 1.

God created man in his own image. Genesis i, 27.

Know ye not that ye are the temple of God, and that the Spirit of God dwelleth in you?

If any man defile the temple of God, him shall God destroy; for the temple of God is holy, which temple ye are. I Corinthians iii, 16, 17.

After this he sat quietly for a long time apparently lost in thought; then this truly penitent one arose, stood beside his wife and vowed that in future he would be a better man, and their home should be happy as in the old days before this false friend took possession.

Tears of happiness were streaming from the little woman's eyes, and our Witch withdrew, thanking God in her heart for this power he had given her.

CHAPTER III.

On reaching home she found a neighbor waiting outside, who entered with her, in the meantime pouring into the ever sympathetic ears her trouble.

She was bewailing over the downfall of her boy who heretofore had been exceptionally dutiful, invariably spending his evening at home, but of late all was changed. He had contracted the card disease with all its adherent vices, which was rapidly developing into a mania. His salary, which was the home support, was being sacrificed on the gambling altar.

Here was more work. The only son and mainstay of a widowed mother fast going to ruin. Yes, something must be done.

Early the following evening the Witch made it her business to pay a visit to the widow about tea time. The son was hurriedly finishing his meal preparatory to starting out for the night, when somehow he changed his mind and stayed at home instead, and our friend, the Witch, knew that in future he would have sufficient strength of will to pass by his old haunt and on home to his waiting loving mother with his earnings in his pocket, which meant more home comforts, more books and evening reading, and happiness to both.

Turn not to the right hand nor to the left: remove thy foot from evil. Proverbs, iv. 27.

The Witch went home well satisfied with her day's work, and that night thought and planned for the good of humanity. Why not venture further into a wider range for action?

She might peddle her songbirds from door to door, and in this capacity gain access into houses where she could more readily acquaint herself with those in need of her assistance.

CHAPTER IV.

The next morning our Witch opened her Bible and read as she was wont to do before any new undertaking. Her eyes rested on these lines :

If ye then, being evil, know how to give good gifts unto your children, how much more shall your Heavenly Father give the Holy Spirit to them that ask him? Luke xi, 13.

She knelt and prayed long and earnestly for an abundance of this Holy Spirit to guide and help her. She took her birds and started out.

I will put my spirit within you, and cause you to walk in my statutes, and ye shall keep my judgments and do them. Ezekiel xxxvi, 27.

Her first stopping place was at a dwelling that stood back some little distance from the street and was surrounded by flowers.

What drew her attention most was the appearance of a little child whose innocent face reminded her that purity still existed. She entered the grounds and rang the bell.

A young woman opened the door and kindly invited her in. The Witch made some remark about the pretty boy outside, when she saw an expression of pain flit over the lady's face. Something wrong here, she thought.

Yes, the child was hers; she had loved not wisely but too well, Her betrayer, a prosperous business man who was as yet unmarried, was allowed to move in the very best of society, but the finger of scorn was pointed at her from all sides.

She was the only daughter of parents who thought very fondly of their lovable grandchild, still felt keenly the disgrace that had been brought upon the hitherto spotless family name.

Does the seventh commandment demand more obedience from one sex than the other? It reads as if it was spoken to both alike. Our Witch learned the man's name and business address, and departed.

CHAPTER V.

She was so in sympathy with this family that she felt in a hurry to get to work, and so signalled a passing car to stop, and entered. It was well filled, but two seats remaining unoccupied she seated herself in one of them.

Presently a little colored girl came in and took the other. A high-bred dame sitting next elevated her aristocratic nose and pulled her skirts aside as if fearing contamination.

Hear ye, and give ear; be not proud; for the Lord hath spoken. Jeremiah xiii, 15.

There is a generation, O how lofty are their eyes! Proverbs xxx, 13.

Behold, I am against thee, O thou most proud, saith the Lord God of Hosts. Jeremiah 1, 31.

Every one that is proud in heart is an abomination to the Lord. Proverbs xvi, 5.

I will cause the arrogancy of the proud to cease, and will lay low the haughtiness of the terrible. Isaiah xiii, 11.

The lofty looks of man shall be humbled, and the haughtiness of men shall be bowed down. Isaiah ii, 11.

Why draw this color line so tightly? What of this outer covering? Have not these people immortal souls which may be white as the whitest; and in many cases, brilliant talents?

The Witch remembered a circumstance where a king of oratory, holding a high official position, was debarred from sitting at table with a ship's crew on account of this same color, which was only a heavier shading; and is not all creation a matter of shadow and coloring?

And hath made of one blood all nations of men for to dwell on all the face of the earth. Acts xvii, 26.

A shabbily dressed woman came in. The stamp of labor was on her gloveless hands, and she looked weary, indeed. But no attention was paid her whatever.

Then came two flashily attired females. No less than five gentlemen arose to offer seats. Were they more in need of rest than this poor laboring woman?

Ah, well! perhaps they were more heavily burdened with their follies than she with her cares.

For once the Witch was too busy with many thoughts to concentrate her mind on any individual in particular, and passed on and out of the car to finish her day's work.

CHAPTER VI.

She went in to a business establishment and made her way to the office. The proprietor, a busy man of the world, was at his desk. He looked in surprise at the cage of birds; a rather unusual place, certainly, to attempt the sale of a bird, the business house of a man without family.

"I have no use for pets myself, and have no one to give them to."

No one? Then memory stirred; he thought of the one whom he had so cruelly wronged, and of his innocent child in disgrace. Why were these new and better impulses taking possession of his mind? He did not know, but the Witch did.

She saw the result of her work a few days later when his marriage notice was published in the paper. Another family put to rights.

CHAPTER VII.

Next, a respectable looking place that might belong to the occupants, for there was not that unkempt appearance about it that is peculiar to rented property.

Our Witch opened the gate and went in. A scowling woman came to the door who looked daggers at the unwelcome peddler, and said she would not have one of those noisy birds in the house.

About this time her tired-looking husband came home from work, and judging from the tirade of abuse heaped upon him, it was evident that she certainly would not tolerate any noise about the premises that she could not make herself.

It was only a matter of time when this quiet, hard-working man would tire of his home life. Husbands with such life partners are not so much to blame if they do prefer the company of other women, the gambling dens and saloons, or any place rather than their homes.

It is better to dwell in a corner of the housetop than with a brawling woman in a wide house. Proverbs xxi, 9.

How many wives, instead of trying to make home attractive, drive happiness away with their cruel tongues?

Who have said with our tongue will we prevail; our lips are our own who is lord over us? Psalms xii, 4.

Hold thy tongue. Amos vi, 10.

The tongue is a fire, a world of iniquity.

It is an unruly evil, full of deadly poison. James iii, 6, 8.

A soft answer turneth away wrath; but grievous words stir up anger.

A wholesome tongue is a tree of life; but perverseness therein is a breach in the spirit. Proverbs xv, 1, 4.

Let all bitterness, and wrath, and anger, and clamor, and evil speaking, be put away from you, with all malice:

And be ye kind one to another, tender hearted, forgiving one another, as even God for Christ's sake hath forgiven you. Ephesians iv, 31, 32.

The Witch is yet at her work. She proceeded on her way, thankful that she has made one less shrew in the world.

CHAPTER VIII.

On her way along she observed a boy sitting on the walk near some shrubbery. He seemed very intent on whatever he was doing. She approached nearer and saw a poor butterfly denuded of its wings lying quivering in his hand, and he was looking at it with the most intense satisfaction.

"My lad, do you know that—

The eyes of the Lord are in every place, beholding the evil and the good. Proverbs xv, 3.

Even a child is known by his doings, whether his work be pure, and whether it be right. Proverbs xx, 11.

"Understand that it is sinful to torment any living thing."

The boy slunk away, realizing for the first time that it was wrong to torture anything so small as a butterfly.

The disposition to torture seems to be inherent with many boys and if allowed to grow on them will in time predominate over all good impulses, and prompt them to commit the most terrible crimes.

For the land is full of bloody crimes, and the city is full of violence. Ezekiel vii, 23.

If they were taught to cultivate will power to subdue these evil impulses what a blessing would be derived! How prone to wickedness is all human nature, and how much we need to pray for help to overcome it!

Watch and pray. Matthew xxvi, 41.

CHAPTER IX.

The Witch noticed a girl in the regulation uniform of white cap and apron marshalling several children. How oft seen in the want column: "A nurse girl who will wear the cap." Why was this head-gear exacted as a badge of servitude? Why ape the Old World customs?

Say unto the king and to the queen, Humble yourselves, sit down; for your principalities shall come down, even the crown of your glory. Jeremiah xiii, 18.
Thus saith the Lord God: Remove the diadem and take off the crown; this shall not be the same; exalt him that is low, and abase him that is high.
I will overturn, overturn, overturn it; and it shall be no more until he come whose right it is; and I will give it him. xxi, 26, 27.
And the Lord alone shall be exalted in that day. Isaiah ii, 11.

Was not this government founded on the principle of equality? Did not the Pilgrim Fathers estimate one good as another if their righteousness was equal? And the distinction was made only between good and evil doers.

A nation that did righteousness, and forsook not the ordinance of their God. Isaiah lviii, 2.
And ye were now turned, and had done right in my sight in proclaiming liberty every man to his neighbor; and ye had made a covenant before me in the house which is called by my name:
But ye turned and polluted my name, and caused every man his servant, and every man his handmaid, whom he had set at liberty at their pleasure, to return, and brought them into subjection, to be unto you for servants and for handmaids. Jeremiah xxxiv, 16, 17.

Then, again, should it not be more essential for these mothers to look more after the morals of the persons who were to be companions for their children and to be less watchful of Mrs. Grundy's edicts?

For the customs of the people are vain.
They are altogether brutish and foolish; the stock is a doctrine of vanities.
They are vanity, and the work of errors; in the time of their visitation they shall perish. Jeremiah x, 3, 8, 15.

The Witch recalled an instance where a distinguished political leader married a sewing woman, and his bride was ostracized from society when it leaked out that she had labored for a livelihood. Had all these aristocrats as clean a record?

Am afraid one's hands would be somewhat soiled by too close investigation.

Ye are they which justify yourselves before men; but God knoweth your hearts. Luke xvi, 15.

For there is nothing covered that shall not be revealed; neither hid, that shall not be known. Luke xii, 2.

For God shall bring every work into judgment with every secret thing, whether it be good or whether it be evil. Ecclesiastes xii, 14.

The just Lord is in the midst thereof; he will not do iniquity; every morning doth he bring his judgment to light, he faileth not. Zephaniah iii, 5.

CHAPTER X.

One day when passing the jail our Witch was moved with an impulse to go inside. The warden allowed her to pass in. Her heart ached for these poor wretches whose faces from behind the bars looked so hopeless and unhappy, and whose blasphemous language chilled her. She longed for the time when :

Every one that nameth the name of Christ depart from iniquity. II Timothy ii, 19.

Who knew but these criminals were as innocent in the light of God's All-Searching Eye as those who less tried have committed less evil?

For all have sinned and come short of the glory of God. Romans iii, 23.
If we say that we have no sin we deceive ourselves, and the truth is not in us. John i, 8.

Some have better childhood memories of good influenc . brought to bear on their susceptible innocence, and would not hum. ity, begot and reared in iniquity, have a natural inclination to evil, . d consequently be pardonable for greater crimes than those of a healthier nourishment? And would not those stronger ones with great mental gifts have more to answer for accordingly than those of weaker natures? Well, it is beyond any human comprehension to execute perfect justice.

Then hear thou from Heaven, thy dwelling place, and forgive, and render unto every man according unto all his ways, whose heart thou knowest; for thou only knowest the hearts of the children of men. II Chronicles vi, 30.
I, the Lord, search the heart, I try the reins, even to give every man according to his ways, and according to the fruit of his doings. Jeremiah xvii, 10.
The judgments of the Lord are true and righteous altogether. Psalms xix, 9.
But why dost thou judge thy brother? Or why doth thou set at nought thy brother? For we shall all stand before the judgment seat of Christ. Let us not therefore judge one another any more; but judge this rather, that no man put a stumbling block or an occasion to fall in his brother's way. Romans xiv, 10, 13.
Thou art inexcusable, O man, whosoever thou art, that judgest; for wherein thou judgest another, thou condemnest thyself. Romans ii, 1.
Judge not, and ye shall not be judged; condemn not, and ye shall not be condemned; forgive, and ye shall be forgiven. Luke vi, 37.
Therefore judge nothing before the time until the Lord come, who both will bring to light the hidden things of darkness, and will make manifest the counsels of the hearts. I Corinthians iv, 5.

But crime will come to an end in that happy time when we will know each other's innermost thoughts.

What a grand and awful time will be the day of judgment, when the Spirit quickens the dust of centuries! Grand for those who have sincerely tried to serve the King !

Who among us shall dwell with everlasting burnings? He that walketh righteously, and speaketh uprightly; he that despiseth the gain of oppressions, that shaketh his hands from holding of bribes, that stoppeth his ears from hearing of blood, and shutteth his eyes from seeing evil: he shall dwell on high; his place of defence shall be the munitions of rocks; bread shall be sure. Isaiah xxxiii, 14, 15, 16.

Blessed are they that keep his testimonies, and that seek him with the whole heart. Psalms cxix, 2.

They that feared the Lord spake often one to another; and the Lord hearkened and heard it, and a book of remembrance was written before him for them that feared the Lord, and that thought upon his name.

And they shall be mine, saith the Lord of Hosts, in that day when I make up my jewels; and I will spare them as a man spareth his own son that serveth him. Malachi iii, 16, 17.

Awful for the hypocrites when God's magnetic eyes burn into their souls. In this way the world of sin will be dissolved, but space, in which we move and have our being, will never be destroyed.

One generation passeth away and another generation cometh; but the earth abideth forever. Ecclesiastes i, 4.

For thus saith the Lord said: The whole land shall be desolate, yet will I not make a full end. Jeremiah iv, 27.

Lift up your eyes to the heavens, and look upon the earth beneath; for the heavens shall vanish away like smoke, and the earth shall wax old like a garment, and they that dwell therein shall die in like manner; but my salvation shall be forever, and my righteousness shall not be abolished. Isaiah li, 6.

Who may abide the day of his coming? And who shall stand when he appeareth? For he is like a refiner's fire. Malachi iii, 2.

Every man's work shall be made manifest; for the day shall declare it, because it shall be revealed by fire; and the fire shall try every man's work of what sort it is. I Corinthians iii, 13.

For our God is a consuming fire. Hebrews xii, 29.

The earth and all the inhabitants thereof are dissolved; I bear up the pillars of it. Psalms lxxv, 3.

All the earth shall be devoured with the fire of my jealousy. Zephaniah iii, 8.

Their flesh shall consume away while they stand upon their feet, and their eyes shall consume away in their holes, and their tongue shall consume away in their mouth. Zechariah xiv, 12.

As wax melteth before the fire, so let the wicked perish at the presence of God. Psalms lxviii, 2.

Therefore the inhabitants of the earth are burned and few men left. Isaiah xxiv, 6.

All the hosts of heaven shall be dissolved, and the heavens shall be rolled together as a scroll. Isaiah xxxiv, 4.

Woe unto you, scribes and pharisees, hypocrites! for ye devour widow's houses, and for a pretense make long prayers. Therefore ye shall receive the greater damnation. Matthew xxiii, 14.

For the congregation of hypocrites shall be desolate, and fire shall consume the tabernacles of bribery. Job xv, 34.

I will bring you into the wilderness of the people, and there will I plead with you face to face.

And there shall ye remember your ways, and all your doings, wherein ye have been defiled; and ye shall loathe yourselves in your own sight for all your evils that ye have committed. Ezekiel xx, 35, 43.

CHAPTER XI.

The Witch was not a regular attendant at any house of worship of any set creed, but preferred ones of lesser grandeur, feeling that she met with more sincerity within. But one Sabbath morning her steps led to one of the largest and most fashionable churches in the city. The ushers were busy seating the well-dressed throng. She slipped along and took a seat by the side of a sumptuously dressed lady who shifted and spread her drapery a little more as a hint to the intruder that her presence was undesirable.

Many haughty glances of derision were shot at the poorly clad stranger who had presumed to come in their midst. She looked about her on the throng.

All is vanity. Ecclesiastes i, 2.

Richly attired matrons, conscious only of their extreme style ; fair young girls, not a whit less extravagantly garbed than their elders, with cramped waists and all the accoutrements belonging to devotees of fashion.

A pity that such fair flowers like the rose could not remain longer in bud, for both fall into decay all too quickly after maturity. But Dame Fashion seems in a hurry and holds to artificial development.

Make not my Father's house a house of merchandise. John ii, 16.

What more was this great display of finery than one way of advertising goods?

Bring no more vain oblations; incense is an abomination unto me; the new moons and Sabbaths, the calling of assemblies, I cannot away with; it is iniquity, even the solemn meeting.

Wash you, make you clean; put away the evil of your doings from before mine eyes; cease to do evil.

Learn to do well; seek judgment, relieve the oppressed, judge the fatherless, plead for the widow.

Come now, and let us reason together, saith the Lord: though your sins be as scarlet they shall be as white as snow; though they be red like crimson, they shall be as wool.

If ye be willing and obedient, ye shall eat the good of the land.

But if ye refuse and rebel, ye shall be devoured. Isaiah i, 13, 16, 17, 18, 19, 20.

Their land also is full of idols; they worship the works of their own hands that which their own fingers have made. Isaiah ii, 8.

The daughters of Zion are haughty, and walk with stretched forth necks and wanton eyes, walking and mincing as they go, and making a tinkling with their feet.

In that day the Lord will take away the bravery of their tinkling ornaments about their feet, and their cauls, and their round tires like the moon.

The chains, and the bracelets, and the mufflers.

The bonnets, the headbands, and the earrings.

The rings.

The changeable suits of apparel, and the mantels, and the wimples, and the crisping pins.

The glasses, and the fine linen, and the hoods, and the vails. Isaiah iii, 16, 18, 19, 20, 21, 22, 23.

That women adorn themselves in modest apparel, with shamefacedness and sobriety; not with broidered hair, or gold, or pearls, or costly array;

But (which becometh women professing godliness) with good works. I Timothy ii, 9, 10.

The eloquent and eminent divine preached a flowery discourse with no reproof pointing to the vanity and frivolity of the hour.

They are shepherds that cannot understand; they all look to their own way, every one for his gain, from his quarter. Isaiah lvi, 11.

Many pastors have destroyed my vineyard; they have trodden my portion under foot. Jeremiah xii, 10.

The pastors are become brutish, and have not sought the Lord. Jeremiah x, 21.

Woe unto you, ye blind guides. Matthew xxiii, 16.

Whose mouths must be stopped, who subvert whole houses, teaching things which they ought not, for filthy lucre's sake. Titus i, 11.

Ye are departed out of the way; ye have caused many to stumble at the law. Malachi ii, 8.

Preach the word; be instant in season, out of season; reprove, rebuke, extort with all long suffering and doctrine.

For the time will come when they will not endure sound doctrine; but after their own lusts shall they heap to themselves teachers having itching ears;

And they shall turn away their ears from the truth, and shall be turned into fables.

But watch thou in all things, endure afflictions, do the work of an evangelist, make full proof of thy ministry. II Timothy iv, 2, 3, 4, 5.

The great organ reverberated through the building. The choir sang of God's love to all creatures alike. Two women sat side by side, and the one of loftier mien bowed her head, and for the first time in her life felt the love of God in her heart; and the Witch went out from church happy, knowing that through her influence one soul was redeemed this Sabbath morning.

CHAPTER XII.

Marching along the road came the Salvation Army. A crowd of juveniles bent on hilarity followed in line, mimicking and ridiculing them. The crowd on the sidewalk jeered, and a high dignitary in church affairs joined his voice with the rest, remarking that this rabble never ought to be allowed to parade the streets Sunday. Who knows how many degraded lives have been elevated by this much ridiculed religious body who do good work in the slums where religion is most needful, and in so doing follow more closely in the footsteps of the Christ than those who spend their energy in striving among themselves for precedence in the public schools and everywhere?

Why all this contention? Should not real Christian worshippers work in harmony?

Have we not all one Father? Hath not one God created us? Malachi ii, 10.

And there was also a strife among them which of them should be accounted the greatest.

But ye shall not be so; but he that is greatest among you, let him be as the younger; and he that is chief, as he that doth serve. Luke xxii, 24, 26.

Do all things without murmurings and disputings. Philippians ii, 14.

Shun profane and vain babblings. II Timothy ii, 16.

Be at peace among yourselves. I Thessalonians v, 13.

Seek peace and pursue it. Psalms xxxiv, 14.

Let nothing be done through strife or vain glory. Philippians ii, 3.

Now the end of the commandment is charity out of a pure heart, and of a good conscience, and of faith unfeigned.

From which some having swerved have turned aside into vain jangling. I Timothy i, 5, 6.

Examine yourselves whether ye be in the faith; prove your own selves. Be of one mind, live in peace. II Corinthians xiii, 5, 11.

Avoid foolish questions, and genealogies, and contentions, and strivings about the law; for they are unprofitable and vain. Titus iii, 9.

For where envying and strife is, there is confusion and every evil work. James iii, 16.

Now I beseech you brethren by the name of the Lord Jesus Christ, that ye all speak the same thing, and that there be no division among you; but that ye be perfectly joined together in the same mind and in the same judgment. I Corinthians i, 10.

I will therefore that men pray everywhere, lifting up holy hands, without wrath and doubting. I Timothy ii, 8.

Behold, ye fast for strife and debate.

Is not this the fast that I have chosen? to loose the bands of wickedness, to undo the heavy burdens, and to let the oppressed go free, and that ye brake every yoke?

Is it not to deal thy bread to the hungry, and that thou bring the poor that are cast out to thy house?

When thou seest the naked that thou cover him; and that thou hide not thyself from thine own flesh?

Then shall thy light break forth as the morning; and thy righteousness shall go before thee; the glory of the Lord shall be thy reward.

Then shalt thou call, and the Lord shall answer; thou shalt cry, and he shall say: Here I am. If thou take away from the midst of thee the yoke, the putting forth of the finger, and speaking vanity;

And if thou draw out thy soul to the hungry and satisfy the afflicted soul; then shall thy light rise in obscurity, and thy darkness be as noonday;

And the Lord shall guide thee continually. Isaiah lviii, 4, 6, 7, 8, 9, 10, 11.

Let us hear the conclusion of the whole matter: Fear God and keep his commandments, for this is the whole duty of man. Ecclesiastes xii, 13.

He hath showed thee, O Man, what is good; and what doth the Lord require of thee but to do justly, and to love mercy, and to walk humbly with thy God? Micah vi, 8.

CHAPTER XIII.

The Witch resumed work Monday morning. There was more stir in the streets than usual. On every corner were groups of excited men. Nothing but whisky and election would cause so much commotion.

The carriages of the different candidates were out scouring the town for voters.

Some of these aspirants for office had almost impoverished themselves by daily treating the crowd of loafers who are always ready to trade their votes for whisky.

They go about electioneering for themselves. Bosh! if a man has the elements of greatness he will find his place without all this self-praise.

For men to search their own glory is not glory. Proverbs xxv, 27.
For if a man think himself to be something, when he is nothing, he deceiveth himself. Galatians vi, 3.

Election day and no mistaking it; the saloons are supposed to be closed, but there is a back door to some of them.

It is not for kings to drink wine; nor for princes strong drink: Lest they drink and forget the law and pervert the judgment of any of the afflicted. Proverbs xxxi, 4, 5.

Is it any wonder that the women of our land clamor for a voice in the affairs of state and nation?

But a woman's place is not at the polls. She can do more good at home in training the minds of her sons, the future voters, and in making her husband's home-coming pleasant, that he may prefer it to haunts of vice. And it is to be hoped that man through debauchery will not become altogether inefficient and make it necessary for woman to take the lead.

But I suffer not a woman to teach nor to usurp authority over the man, but to be in silence. I Timothy ii, 12.

CHAPTER XIV.

In the evening at that most entrancing hour between daylight and dark, when all creation seems in a dreamy mood, the Witch found herself at the entrance of a gilded palace of sin. A number of the inmates were flitting about the flower-laden, well-kept grounds. She approached one of exquisite beauty of person whose face was not yet passion-scarred.

She was dressed in some soft, flowing, white material which gave her more of a seraphic appearance than one of sensualism. The Witch asked what brought her to this stage of immorality. The woman's reply was that she had been reared in wealth, but her father through some unlucky speculation lost everything. She had never learned to work, but had been taught that any labor was most degrading, and she had not qualified herself to teach any branch of learning, never having made allowance for the swift wings of vanishing wealth.

When thrown on her own resources she was at a loss to know what to do, when a wealthy gentleman friend came to her assistance at the sacrifice of her honor.

He soon tired of her, however; her father had died broken-hearted, and her mother was staying with a distant relative who had kindly offered her a home.

The Witch persuaded her to leave this life of disgrace, to learn honest work and brighten her mother's remaining years.

Study to show thyself approved unto God, a workman that needeth not to be ashamed. II Timothy ii, 15.

She said that it would be hard for her to face the world with this stigma of shame on her character; that all those bearing any claim to respectability would scorn her.

The Witch told her that God was judge and not the people, and their lives were not altogether blameless.

God is the judge. Psalms lxxv, 7.
He that is without sin among you, let him first cast a stone at her. John viii, 7.

The woman was undecided, but the better mind prevailed and she accompanied the Witch home, and the next day found respectable employment.

And still the good work goes on.

Reader, I am only narrating a small portion of this woman's work which she found as the days went by to be illimitable. *Vice versa.* If one possessing this mysterious power was inclined to evil rather than good, what a great amount of wickedness might be accomplished through it. God only knows how much of the good and evil that has been done in the world may be attributed to this hidden force.

Was the famed enchantress of the Nile gifted with this secret to a very great extent, and many other characters of history celebrated in their day for the influence they exercised?

CHAPTER XV.

The Witch heard of a murder trial that was going on in court and arousing intense interest, owing to the high social standing of all the parties concerned. She acted on impulse to a certain extent and, leaving her birds at home, started at once for the court-house.

On her way there she turned her attention to a case of street pugilism. A crowd of boys, ranging in age from seven to twenty, had congregated. Two small urchins were fighting; their faces were scratched and bleeding, and the crowd was urging them on to do each other more injury.

These young ruffians made a study of wickedness which is more than mischief, and this element is on an increase the world over.

Yea also the heart of the sons of men is full of evil. Ecclesiastes ix, 3.

No wonder when they have for examples men in high places who take such interest in prize fighting.

It would be more in keeping with their positions if their minds could aspire to something more elevating. They are ready enough to censure the Spaniards for their bull fights, but are themselves not far in advance when they will encourage this barbarous sport which seems to be gaining popularity.

The wicked walk on every side when the vilest men are exalted. Psalms xii, 8.

For the leaders of this people cause them to err; and they that are led of them are destroyed. Isaiah ix, 16.

These are the men that devise mischief and give wicked counsel in this city. Ezekiel xi, 2.

If they would exercise the spiritual nature more and the animal less they could take no pleasure in such brutish doing.

For the flesh lusteth against the Spirit, and the Spirit against the flesh; and these are contrary the one to the other. Galatians v, 17.

Even the Press takes a hand in it, and devotes whole columns of the papers to explaining in minutest detail the movements of the combatants.

Our Witch was wrapped in thought, but did not forget her work, and in a few moments after she appeared among them the shamefaced crowd dispersed.

CHAPTER XVI.

When the chief witness against the accused was called to give his testimony there was one among the throng of spectators whose eyes never left his face.

He started in a resolute manner, then wavered a little, and finally broke down in the midst of it and confessed his own guilt. He was the murderer.

Thou shalt not bear false witness against thy neighbor. Exodus xx, 16.
Confess your faults one to another, and pray one for another. James v, 16.
He that covereth his sins shall not prosper; but whoso confesseth and forsaketh them shall have mercy. Proverbs xxviii, 13.
If we confess our sins he is faithful and just to forgive us our sins, and to cleanse us from all unrighteousness. John i, 9.

There was a hush like the hush of death in the courtroom while he was speaking. When the crowd passed out, a plainly garbed figure went out also unobserved. The Witch had done her work for the day.

CHAPTER XVII.

She looked on the cars gliding over the electric road. What of this occult power? And what of her own? Eventually would electricity impel the entire universe?

Had this always existed and was yet to be brought out by masterful minds? Was this the connecting link between God and man? Then it was wisely said in ages past :

How long, ye simple ones, will ye love simplicity? Proverbs i, 22.

The Lord possessed me in the beginning of his way before his works of old.

When he prepared the heavens I was there; when he set a compass upon the face of the depth. Proverbs vii, 22, 27.

He ruleth by his power forever. Psalms lxvi, 7.

In the Lord Jehovah is everlasting strength. Isaiah xxvi, 4.

Take hold of my strength. Isaiah xxvii, 5.

Have ye not known? have ye not heard? hath it not been told you from the beginning? have ye not understood from the foundation of the earth? Isaiah xl, 21, 22.

For my people is foolish; they have not known me; they are sottish children, and they have none understanding; they are wise to do evil, but to do good they have no knowledge. Jeremiah iv, 22.

Understand, ye brutish among the people, and ye fools, when will ye be wise? Psalms xciv, 8.

O ye simple, understand wisdom; and ye fools, be ye of an understanding heart. Proverbs viii, 5.

Yea, if thou criest after knowledge, and liftest up thy voice for understanding;

If thou seekest her as silver, and searchest for her as for hid treasures;

Then shalt thou understand the fear of the Lord, and find the knowledge of God. Proverbs ii. 3, 4, 5.

He hath made the earth by his power, he hath established the world by his wisdom, and hath stretched out the heavens by his discretion.

When he uttereth his voice, there is a multitude of waters in the heavens, and he causeth the vapors to ascend from the ends of the earth; he maketh lightnings with rain, and bringeth forth the wind out of his treasures. Jeremiah x, 12, 13.

The heavens declare the glory of God; and the firmament sheweth his handiwork.

Day unto day uttereth speech, and night unto night sheweth knowledge.

There is no speech nor language where their voice is not heard.

Their line is gone out through all the earth, and their words to the end of the world. In them hath he set a tabernacle for the sun,

Which is as a bridegroom coming out of his chamber, and rejoiceth as a strong man to run a race.

His going forth is from the ends of the heaven, and his circuit unto the ends of it, and there is nothing hid from the heat thereof. Psalms xix, 1, 2, 3, 4, 5, 6.

The voice of the Lord is upon the waters; the God of glory thundereth, the Lord is upon many waters.

The voice of the Lord is powerful. xxix, 3, 4.

The thunder of his power who can understand? Job xxvi, 14.

With thee is the fountain of life; in thy light shall we see light. Psalms xxxvi, 9.

The earth shall be filled with the knowledge of the glory of the Lord, as the waters cover the sea. Habakkuk ii, 14.

Who is wise, and will observe these things, even they shall understand. Psalms cvii, 43.

At the resurrection, when the Lamb of God will rule the world as the center of gravitation like the sun, who among us can study mischief in secret when mind meets mind in one common thoroughfare of thought which cannot be divided by land or sea?

As the lightning cometh out of the east, and shineth even unto the west; so shall also the coming of the Son of Man be. Matthew xxiv, 27.

And the city hath no creed of the sun, neither of the moon, to shine in it; for the glory of God did lighten it, and the Lamb is the light thereof. Revelation xxi, 23.

The sun shall be no more thy light by day; neither for brightness shall the moon give light unto thee; but the Lord shall be unto thee an everlasting light, and thy God thy glory.

Thy sun shall no more go down; neither shall thy moon withdraw itself; for the Lord shall be thine everlasting light. Isaiah lx, 19, 20.

There shall be a resurrection of the dead, both of the just and unjust. Acts xxiv, 15.

As the Father raiseth up the dead and quickeneth them, even so the Son quickeneth whom he will. John v, 21.

Ye shall know that I am the Lord, when I have opened your graves, O my people, and brought you up out of your graves.

And shall put my spirit in you, and ye shall live. Ezekiel xxxvii, 13, 14.

The dead men shall live together; with my dead body shall they arise.

Awake and sing, ye that dwell in dust; for thy dew is as the dew of herbs, and the earth shall cast out the dead. Isaiah xxvi, 19.

CHAPTER XVIII.

One morning when near a handsome residence the Witch stopped at the sound of a musical instrument. The music ceased and a lady of forty or thereabout answered her ring.

She was surrounded with every luxury, but our Witch soon learned that here, too, was trouble. Yes, another mismated couple.·

The lady said that her husband and herself had never lived very happily together after the first few months of married life; and recently another woman had come between them, and her husband, desirous of a separation, was about to commence proceedings for a divorce from her. As for herself it mattered little, but for the sake of her children she had rather it would not be.

Presently the husband came. He was a fine-looking man of pleasing address and unless appearance was deceiving he would do very well if started on the right track.

Here was more work for the ever busy brain.

Lo, this only have I found, that God hath made man upright; but they have sought out many inventions. Ecclesiastes vii, 29.

Yet I had planted thee a noble vine, wholly a right seed; how then art thou turned into the degenerate plant of a strange vine unto me ? Jeremiah ii, 21.

He sat down facing the Witch, and after a little time was conscious of a new train of thoughts. His better spirit moved. Would it not be as well to live the remainder of his life with the mother of his children whom he dearly loved ?

What therefore God hath joined together let not man put asunder. Matthew xix, 6.

Contract marriage is most suitable for the present age. That leaves the contracting parties on a grade with the cattle and admits of their changing companions whenever and as often as they like without breaking God's holy vows.

And this have ye done again, covering the altar of the Lord with tears, with weeping, and with crying out, insomuch that he regardeth not the offering any more, or receive it with good will at your hand.

Because the Lord hath been witness between thee and the wife of thy youth, against whom thou hast dealt treacherously; yet is she thy companion and the wife of thy covenant.

And did not he make one? yet had he the residue of the spirit.

Therefore take heed to your spirit, and let none deal treacherously against the wife of his youth.

For the Lord, the God of Israel, saith that he hateth putting away. Malachi ii, 13, 14, 15, 16.

If a man put away his wife and she go from him, and become another man's, shall not that land be greatly polluted? Jeremiah iii, 1.

When a marriage is solemnized by the word of God, then no law on earth is justifiable for breaking it; and when a couple truly love each other what but death can separate them? For misfortune of any kind only binds the tie of sympathy more closely.

If this tie was not so easily broken more persons would consider whom they were marrying and what they were marrying for, and if less deception was practiced beforehand, there would be fewer marriages which prove such dismal failures.

The heart is deceitful above all things, and desperately wicked; who can know it? Jeremiah xvii, 9.

We will be done with all this in the resurrection.

In the resurrection they neither marry, nor are given in marriage, but are as the angels of God in heaven. Matthew xxii, 30.

When the Witch left this pair she was happy in the thought that they would live together on better terms, and be like a re-united family.

CHAPTER XIX.

Later in the day our Witch was in another part of the city; while walking through an alley, she saw a Chinaman carrying a large basket full of clean clothes that he was returning to the owners. The Witch also noticed several half-grown boys and heard one of them remark:

"Say we take a shot at that heathen."

So with one accord they commenced pelting him with everything available. Their victim tried to defend himself to the best of his ability, but the half dozen boys pounced on him, and in the fracas the clothes were upset into the street.

It was hard to tell how far they would carry their vicious work, which they considered a capital joke, when some one appeared among them who was also at work. Very soon they all left off, not knowing why. The Witch stood near while he gathered up the clothes, which necessarily must be washed over again.

Then she tried to solve in her mind this Chinese problem:

These Mongolians are in a measure obnoxious, but as a rule are peaceable and industrious, which is more than can be said of many other people.

They have few opportunities for making a living in their own over-populous country, but perhaps when they have become more thoroughly Christianized, the race will be less prolific, which would be beneficial to their own nation and others.

Say among the heathen that the Lord reigneth. Psalms xcvi, 10.

For the more a man leans to divinity the less he cleaves to his animal nature; and what is true of the Chinese applies to other densely populated countries.

For they that are after the flesh do mind the things of the flesh; but they that are after the Spirit, the things of the Spirit. Romans viii, 5.

Let not sin therefore reign in your mortal body, that ye should obey it in the lusts thereof. Romans vi, 12.

For all that is in the world, the lust of the flesh, and the lust of the eyes, and the pride of life, is not of the Father, but is of the world.

And the world passeth away, and the lust thereof; but he that doeth the will of God abideth forever. John ii, 16, 17.

Her mind reverted to an incident which she witnessed in a cemetery. It was the Sabbath and she was walking about in there as she often did on this day, for what more forcible sermon can be delivered than a thinking mind can feel while moving about among the dead?

After a time she was conscious of a disturbance of some kind going on at one corner of the enclosure. A promiscuous crowd had gathered and ere long there came a Chinese funeral train and stopped at the open grave.

Then the crowd mocked them, and by this time it was evident that they had gathered there to have sport at the expense of the mourners.

The children were cutting up all manner of antics, and the parents stood by highly amused at the proceedings. It was almost impossible to conduct the burial rites on account of the confusion made by the mob.

To be sure it was a peculiar ceremony, but some respect ought to have been due the feelings of these sorrowing ones at such a time. These children were wholly undisciplined in the matter of right and wrong; their behavior was like so many young savages.

What were their parents teaching them? To selfishly enjoy the discomfort of others, and this was all, never trying to encourage the finer and better feelings in their natures.

Our Witch did not wait till the ceremony was over. Thoroughly disgusted with human nature, she left the cemetery.

CHAPTER XX.

She thought still less of it that night when awakened from sleep by a gang of boisterous picnickers who, full of liquor, were returning home from a day of revelry. Women's and men's voices mingled together in singing vile songs.

How wholly depraved are some natures, and how necessary that these lewd minds should be purified by a closer communion with more spiritual intellects !

When there are seven days in a week and our King only exacts from us the Sabbath it does seem as if He is entitled to that, but where people are confined to employment every day in the week but one, it is hardly probable that the kind Father would object to their having an outing on their one day of liberty out of a week of unremitting toil, if they would conduct themselves properly.

Not in rioting and drunkenness; not in chambering and wantonness. But put ye on the Lord Jesus Christ, and make not provision for the flesh to fulfill the lusts thereof. Romans xiii, 13, 14.

My Sabbaths they greatly polluted.

I am the Lord your God; walk in my statutes, and hallow my Sabbaths. Ezekiel xx, 13.

Thus saith the Lord, keep ye judgment, and do justice.

Blessed is the man that doeth this, and the son of man that layeth hold on it; that keepeth the Sabbath from polluting it, and keepeth his hand from doing any evil. Isaiah lvi, 1, 2.

If thou turn away thy foot from the Sabbath, from doing thy pleasure on my holy day; and call the Sabbath a delight, the holy of the Lord, honorable; and shalt honour him, not doing thine own ways, nor finding thine own pleasure, nor speaking thine own words:

Then shalt thou delight thyself in the Lord; and I will cause thee to ride upon the high places of the earth, and feed thee with the heritage of Jacob thy father; for the mouth of the Lord hath spoken it. Isaiah lviii, 13, 14.

But ere long a few cannot monopolize all the comforts, nor the masses be obliged to struggle hard every hour for the bare necessities of life, for who can defraud his neighbor when all minds will be a unit? and if honesty was practiced to the letter, the good things of life would not be so unequally divided.

The profit of the earth is for all. Ecclesiastes v, 9.

Yet ye say, the way of the Lord is not equal. Is not my way equal? Are not your ways unequal? Ezekiel xviii, 25.

For every one from the least even unto the greatest is given to covetousness, from the prophet even unto the priest, every one dealeth falsely. Jeremiah viii, 10.

Their tongue is an arrow shot out; it speaketh deceit; one speaketh peaceably to his neighbor with his mouth, but in heart he layeth wait. Jeremiah ix, 8.

As a cage is full of birds, so are their houses full of deceit; therefore they are become great, and waxen rich. Jeremiah v, 27.

Behold these are the ungodly who prosper in the world; they increase in riches. Psalms lxxiii, 12.

Thus saith the Lord, execute ye judgment and righteousness, and deliver the spoiled out of the hand of the oppressor; and do no wrong, do no violence to the stranger, the fatherless, nor the widow. Jeremiah xxii, 3.

Be renewed in the spirit of your mind; putting away lying, speak every man truth with his neighbor; for we are members one of another. Ephesians iv, 23, 25.

That they all may be one; as thou, Father, art in me, and I in thee, that they also may be one in us. John xvii. 21.

Behold, how good and how pleasant it is for brethren to dwell together in unity! Psalms cxxxiii, 1.

CHAPTER XXI.

Ever on the alert to do good the Witch stopped at a rickety tenement, with nothing to recommend it but a climbing rose-bush, set out by some flower-loving tenant a number of years before, and which twined its long branches in full bloom over one end of the dilapidated structure; it was an illustration of extremes meeting, this perfectly beautiful rose-bush and the unsightly old porch. The landlady did not care to buy a bird, and none of the occupants of her rooms were at home during the day, except one, who poor boy, was always in, and a visitor would be sure to cheer him up a bit, though it would be useless to try and sell a bird there. She led the way up a flight of stairs to the room where a little cripple was amusing himself with a few marbles that he was rolling about on the table by which he was sitting.

He was delighted with the birds, but knew that his sister could not afford to buy him one. He said she was employed up town in a store, naming the business block of a well-known and very wealthy merchant, and he could not go out and play like other boys, and the days seemed very long sometimes.

Yes, thought our Witch, a day must be a long time to this poor weakling with little to amuse him.

She gave him his choice of the birds, and after promising to bring it back in the evening with a new cage which she would buy for him, the Witch took her leave.

CHAPTER XXII.

A little way down the street in advance of her was a heavy wagon drawn by one patient horse that looked as though it might have seen better days, but now one could numerate every rib in its worn frame. The driver was beating the poor animal unmercifully. It doubtless had a history, and if allowed speech would tell of a gradual decline, of careful nourishment and little to do in its prime, but when strength and beauty began to wane, of a harder life, and now in old age when attention was most needful, must fall in line with the great majority of overworked, under-fed beasts of burden, and some day when no longer able to hold up the harness, would be taken out and shot.

Our Witch could hear in her mind's ear the rebuke of old :

What have I done unto thee, that thou has smitten me these three times ? Numbers xxii, 28.

She watched the man intently for a few seconds, and then his arm dropped to his side. Why this sudden sympathy so foreign to his hardened nature ?

The All-seeing Eye must often look down in tenderest pity on this ill-treated animal creation, which is more deserving of His regard than these inhuman beings, who by their cruelty place themselves far below a level with the lower animals.

The Lord is good to all ; and His tender mercies are over all His works. Psalms cxlv, 9.

Be ye therefore merciful, as your Father is also merciful. Luke vi, 36.

The merciful man doeth good to his own soul : but he that is cruel troubleth his own flesh. Proverbs xi, 17.

Surely the Society for the Prevention of Cruelty to Animals is one of the noblest organizations of modern times, and for good work stands second to no religious denomination that has ever existed, or ever will exist.

CHAPTER XXIII.

Her next stopping place was not in a rookery part of the city, but was where wealth abounds. It was just before the noon hour when she entered the palatial home of a many times millionaire and was ushered into the library where he was busy with some papers. "Would you care to buy a bird, sir?"

"I have no time to talk with you this morning, madam." He looked at her uneasily, and mentally resolved to administer a reproof to the servant for allowing these tramping peddlars to enter the house.

The magnetic power was again brought into requisition.

The Witch might have used this influence for her own financial advantage, but was too concientious for that, and furthermore money was not her aim in life.

Gradually there came stealing into this rich man's brain new thoughts; was he doing right with his boundless wealth? He could not understand why he was just waking up to the fact that he had not.

How many needy ones had he passed by?

Withhold not good to them to whom it is due, when it is in the power of thine hand to do it. Proverbs iii, 27.

To endow some charitable institution at his death, as a monument to his own memory, would hardly atone for neglected duty. Would God hold him responsible for this neglect and bar him from the Kingdom?

Thou art weighed in the balances, and art found wanting. Daniel v, 27.

Woe unto him that buildeth his house by unrighteousness, and his chambers by wrong; that useth his neighbor's service without wages, and giveth him not for his work. Thine eyes and thine heart are not but for thy covetousness. Jeremiah xxii, 13, 17.

Your riches are corrupted, and your garments are moth-eaten. Your gold and silver is cankered; and the rust of them shall be a witness against you and shall eat your flesh as it were fire. Ye have heaped treasures together for the last days. Behold the hire of the laborers who have reaped down your fields, which is of you kept back by fraud, crieth: and the cries of them which reaped are entered into the ears of the Lord of Sabaoth. James v, 2, 3, 4.

Who so stoppeth his ears at the cry of the poor, he shall cry himself, but shall not be heard.   Proverbs xxi, 13.

Let not the rich man glory in his riches.   Jeremiah ix, 23.

Neither their silver nor their gold shall be able to deliver them in the day of the Lord's wrath.   Zephaniah i, 18.

Charge them that are rich in this world, that they be not high-minded, nor trust in uncertain riches, but in the living God, who giveth us richly all things to enjoy.   That they do good, that they be rich in good works, ready to distribute.   I Timothy vi, 17, 18.

He that oppresseth the poor reproacheth his Maker: but he that honoreth Him hath mercy on the poor.   Proverbs xiv, 31.

As a partridge sitteth on eggs, and hatcheth them not; so he that getteth riches, and not by right, shall leave them in the midst of his days, and at his end shall be a fool.   Jeremiah xvii, 11.

CHAPTER XXIV.

Faithful to her promise, the Witch purchased a cage, and early in the evening returned to the cripple's abode and was joyfully greeted. "O, but you are a good lady to think of me, only a cripple boy!" She felt that it was indeed more blessed to give than to receive (Acts XX, 35) when one could do God a service at the same time.

As ye have done it unto the least of these ye have done it unto Me. Matthew xxv, 40.

He that hath pity upon the poor lendeth to the Lord. Proverbs xix, 17.

In a short time the sister came. His face brightened up with pleasure when he told her of the present he had received; now he would have a companion all through the long days.

She was also in a happy mood. The head of the firm where she worked had raised the salary of all his employes, and she was very thankful for her good luck because of her brother who needed more books and toys, for the poor child had to amuse himself the best he could during the day. The Witch returned home. She saw the progress of her work many times after in this millionaire's acts of benevolence which were so liberal as to excite press comment.

Blessed is he that considereth the poor; the Lord will deliver him in time of trouble. Psalms xli, 1.

CHAPTER XXV.

Our Witch read of the doings in the old world and was sorry that distance and sea prevented this influence from being brought to bear upon some of the crowned heads, who, born to almost absolute power, showed no mercy to a religious sect, who according to Holy Writ are the chosen people of God. But one alone cannot revolutionize the earth, unless that one be omnipotent.

Some day this persecution must come to an end.

For the Lord will have mercy on Jacob, and will yet choose Israel, and set them in their own land, and the stranger shall be joined with them. Isaiah xiv, 1.

Prepare to meet thy God, O Israel. Amos iv, 12.

The great day of the Lord is near, it is near, and hasteth greatly. Zephaniah i, 14.

Let all the inhabitants of the land tremble, for the day of the Lord cometh, for it is nigh at hand. Joel, ii, 1.

But of that day and hour no man, no not the angels of heaven, but my Father only. Watch, therefore, for ye know not what hour your Lord doth come. Matthew xxiv, 36, 42.

Obey, I beseech thee, the voice of the Lord, which I speak unto thee, so it shall be well unto thee, and thy soul shall live. Jeremiah xxxviii, 20.

Return ye now every one from his evil way and make your ways and your doings good. Jeremiah xviii, 11.

And to wait for his Son from heaven whom he raised from the dead, even Jesus, which delivered us from the wrath to come. I Thessalonians i, 10.

Neither is there salvation in any other; for there is none other name under heaven given among men, whereby we must be saved. Acts iv, 12.

There is therefore now no condemnation to them which are in Christ Jesus who walk not after the flesh, but after the Spirit. Romans viii, 1.

Draw nigh to God and he will draw nigh to you;

Cleanse your hands, ye sinners, and purify your hearts, ye double minded. James iv, 8.

Behold, I stand at the door and knock: if any man hear my voice, and open the door, I will come in to him, and will sup with him, and he with me. Revelation iii, 20.

I will heal their backsliding, I will love them freely. Hosea xiv, 4.

Repent ye, therefore, and be converted, that your sins may be blotted out when the times of refreshing shall come from the presence of the Lord; and he shall send Jesus Christ, which before was preached unto you. Acts iii, 19, 20.

If ye thoroughly amend your ways and your doings; if ye thoroughly execute judgment between a man and his neighbor;

If ye oppress not the stranger, the fatherless, and the widow, and shed not innocent blood in this place, neither walk after other gods to your hurt;

Then will I cause you to dwell in this place, in the land I gave to your fathers, for ever and ever. Obey my voice and I will be your God, and ye shall be my people. Jeremiah vii, 5, 6, 7, 23.

Therefore, turn thou to thy God; keep mercy and judgment, and wait on thy God continually. Hosea xii, 6.

Depart from evil and do good, and dwell for evermore. Psalms xxxvii, 27.

The redeemed of the Lord shall return, and come singing unto Zion; and everlasting joy shall be upon their head; they shall obtain gladness and joy; and sorrow and mourning shall flee away. Isaiah li, 11.

And it shall come to pass that he that is left in Zion, and he that remaineth in Jerusalem shall be called holy, even every one that is written among the living in Jerusalem. When the Lord shall have washed away the filth of the daughters of Zion, and shall have purged the blood of Jerusalem from the midst thereof by the spirit of judgment, and by the spirit of burning. Isaiah iv, 3, 4.

Behold, I come quickly. And the Spirit and the bride say, come; and let him that heareth say, come; and let him that is athirst come; and whosoever will, let him take the water of life freely. Revelation xxii, 7, 17.

CHAPTER XXVI.

The Witch did not go about her work the next day, nor the next, for somehow she contracted a severe cold which completely prostrated her, and then pneumonia clutched her throat.

One morning, when the first golden rays of the sun glanced over the sleeping city, they rested in benediction on her death bed. A neighbor, whom in time past she had befriended, was at her side.

She knew that the end was near.

Will this influence stop here? or will it go on and on through all the ages to come?

Blessed are the dead which die in the Lord from henceforth: Yea, saith the Spirit, that they may rest from their labours; and their works do follow them.   Revelation xiv, 13.

www.ingramcontent.com/pod-product-compliance
Lightning Source LLC
Chambersburg PA
CBHW020817030726
47496CB00009B/2924